More than 500 things to spot

TOTALLY AWESOME

EXPLORE AND FIND

This edition published by Cottage Door Press, LLC in 2021.

First published 2014 by Parragon Books, Ltd.

Copyright © 2021 Cottage Door Press, LLC
5005 Newport Drive
Rolling Meadows, Illinois 60008

Cover illustrated by Steve Wood
Illustrated by Lorna Anderson, Isabel Aniel, Jean Claude, Genie Espinosa,
Brian Fitzgerald, Emily Golden, Megan Higgins, Gareth Lucas, Samantha Meredith,
Ed Meyer, Sophie Rohrbach, Craig Shuttlewood, Steve Wood, and Jordan Wray

ISBN 978-1-64638-309-2

Parragon Books is an imprint of Cottage Door Press, LLC.
Parragon Books® and the Parragon® logo are registered trademarks of Cottage Door Press, LLC.

TOTALLY AWESOME
EXPLORE AND FIND

More than **500** things to spot

PaRragon.

Let's go animal spotting in the jungle! Find ...

3 tree frogs

3 caterpillars

1 chameleon

4 toucans

 2 lion monkeys

 2 purple lizards

 1 dragonfly

 2 parrots

There's lots to spot in the snowy farmyard. Find ...

1 award

3 blue hats

3 sheep

1 fox

1 striped yellow scarf

3 robins

1 rooster

1 bull

Beep, beep! The busy city has a lot of traffic. Find ...

1 purple car

2 dogs

6 taxis

1 delivery van

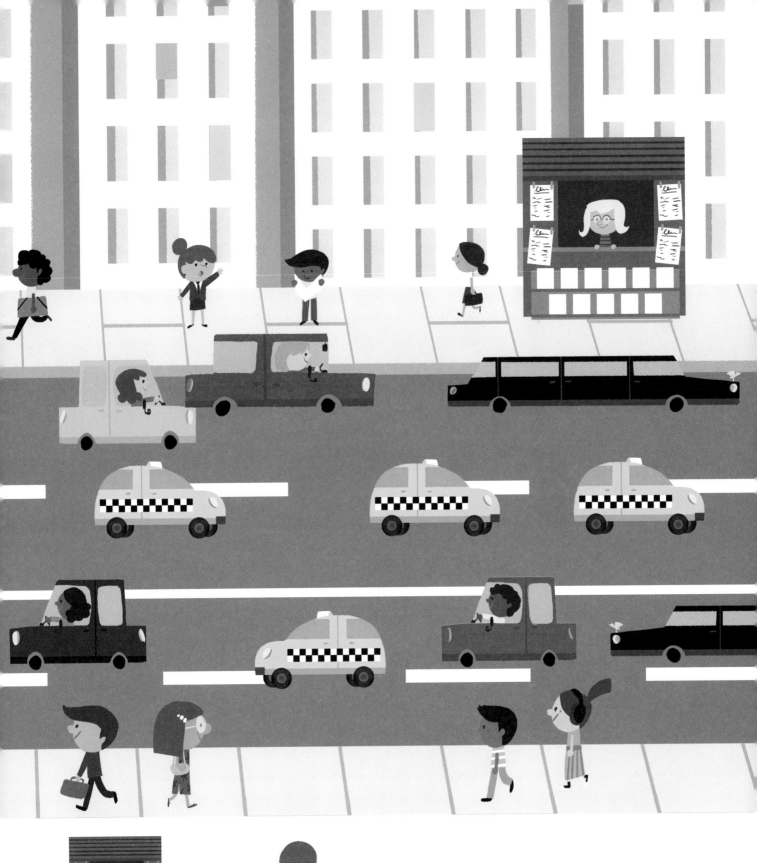

1 newspaper stand

1 red balloon

1 pink car

2 green cars

How many creatures can you count?

Find these sea creatures in the coral reef.

3 shrimp

4 clownfish

6 crabs

1 octopus

There's so much to see on safari! Find ...

2 meerkats

2 monkeys

1 cheetah

3 red snakes

1 pink bird

2 ostriches

1 dung beetle

3 toucans

Find each of these things on the mountain.

Flower power!

Find each of these flowers in the park.

There are so many ways to travel! Find ...

3 submarines

2 scooters

2 helicopters

1 yellow train

1 hot air balloon

1 seaplane

1 sailboat

1 cruise ship

It's a busy day at the sweet factory! Find ...

1 heart cookie

1 penguin

1 green boot

1 pink ice cream

1 lion

1 purple pot

1 bottle of
green sauce

1 bottle of
blue sauce

Help the poor pirates find their things.

ship's cat

deck of cards

pirate hat

Jolly Roger flag

Find the 5 green machines with blue wheels.

It's an alien planet! Find ...

2 red aliens

5 green aliens

2 red rockets

3 blue aliens

2 yellow spaceships

1 purple alien

1 blue planet

1 space rover

Let's go bug spotting! Find ...

5 ladybugs

2 pink bugs

6 grasshoppers

3 spiders

2 red butterflies

3 blue bugs

3 bumblebees

Crash! Bang! What a busy building site. Find ...

1 cement truck

1 cement mixer

1 spaceship

1 space alien

1 excavator

2 wheelbarrows

1 builder in a red hat

1 truck

There's a traffic jam in the town! Find ...

8 ducks

1 taxi

1 stretch limo

1 sports car

5 lamp posts

1 hot dog stand

1 roller skater

1 apple tree

Lots of animals are busy burrowing! Find ...

1 crown

3 bugs

1 red hard hat

1 badger

5 foxes

2 bumblebees

2 ladybugs

2 diamonds

Join in the prehistoric playtime! Find ...

1 green lizard

1 swimming dino

1 red dino

1 orange dino

1 green dino

1 hatching egg

1 purple dino

1 blue dino

How many aliens are swooping around in space?

Find 8 happy pumpkins!

Life is sweet. Find ...

3 sprinkle ice pops

2 strawberry cones

3 mint cones

2 double cones

2 sundaes   3 red ice pops   4 chocolate-covered cones   3 cups

Find each of these in the playground.

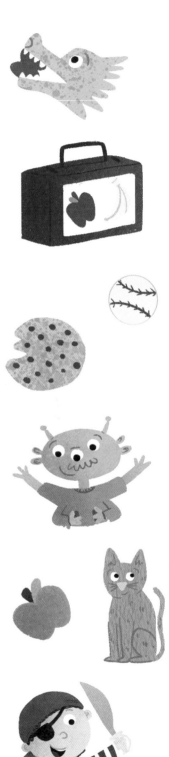

The ocean is full of life! Find ...

1 blue fish

1 orange fish

2 green fish

2 jellyfish

3 striped fish

1 pink fish

2 seahorses

3 starfish

Spot 5 matching pairs of skis in the pile.

How many ghosts can you see in this haunted hallway?

Autumn has come to the farmyard. Find...

1 umbrella

5 pigs

3 rabbits

8 sheep

3 cows

1 rainbow

6 carrots

1 horse

Splish-splash at the seashore! Find ...

1 tortoise

1 bowl of fruit

1 red crab

1 basket of towels

3 beach balls

1 blue ice cream

1 penguin

1 seagull

Up, up, and away!

Find one of each of these kites.

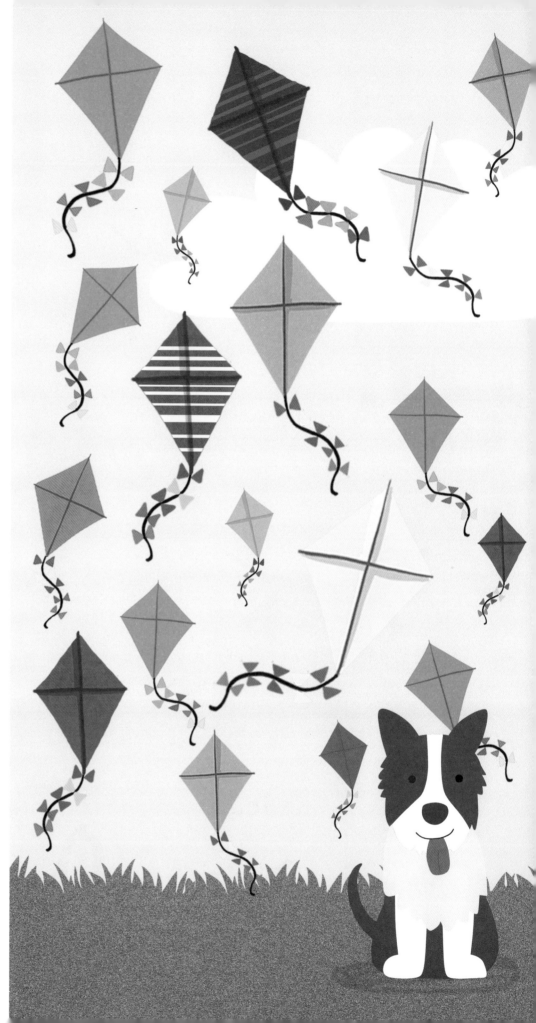

Can you spot 5 rabbits playing with these dogs and cats?

How many
dinosaurs are hiding
in the jungle?

Let's look around the aquarium! Find ...

1 pink fish

1 orange seahorse

1 purple fish

3 turtles

2 octopuses

4 starfish

2 pink jellyfish

1 stingray

A

B

book

C

Library

57

The sun is shining on Apple Tree Farm. Find ...

2 mice

1 sock

3 pigs

4 butterflies

1 ladybug

1 bicycle

3 bees

1 fox

Can you spot 5 sleeping ducks?

Find 5 spotty dinosaurs!

Find these umbrellas before they blow away!

2 red   **2 green**   **2 purple**   **5 blue**

2 yellow **2 pink** **3 orange** **3 gray**

Find each of these friends in the royal kingdom.

How many pink balloons are flying in the sky?

Find each of these objects in the science lab.

Find 11 matching pairs of objects in the ship's storeroom.

Dozy the dog is dreaming of his favorite part of the rug. Can you find it?

CINEMA

SPY DOGS
2

Cafe

SHOE STORE

72

Find each of these secret agents working undercover in the shopping mall.

Looking good! Find ...

 2 green glasses

4 yellow glasses

 3 purple glasses

2 blue glasses

2 orange glasses

3 red glasses

2 white glasses

2 pink glasses

It's market day in Ancient Rome! Find ...

12 gold coins

1 blue vase

1 shield

2 swords

4 houses

1 bale of hay

1 orange fish

1 necklace

How many fish can you find in the fishbowl?

Shhhh, keep quiet and find these four rare birds!

Our city will always be safe! Find ...

 1 green hero

 2 semicircle windows

 3 giraffes

 1 flamingo

1 pink hero

2 red buses

1 purple hero

4 trees

What's cooking? Find each of these things in the kitchen.

Let's watch the big air show! Find ...

4 crates

6 pink flags

3 green planes

2 red banners

1 helicopter

5 blue caps

1 pink plane

5 striped flags

Watch out, coming through! Find ...

10 cones

1 beach ball

1 tent

1 purple ATV

1 dolphin

1 photographer

1 dog

2 yellow helmets

Find each of these birds in the busy tree.

Find each of these ocean explorers.

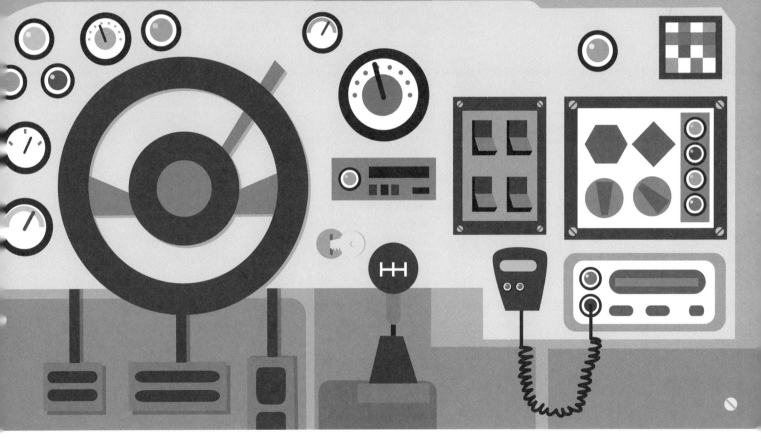

Let's get this car started! Find ...

Quick, we need to stop this leak! Find ...

1 pressure gauge

3 gold rings

1 saw

1 cow

1 tap

1 green hat

1 mug

1 yellow boot

This city lights up at night! Find ...

1 wanted poster

3 clocks

1 police helicopter

1 bull in a hard hat

 2 dogs with flashlights  **1 pirate ship**  **1 shooting star**  **2 police cars**

Help Chris find his friends on the crowded bus.

Find 12 acorns hidden in the woods.

Above and below! Find ...

3 dolphins

1 shark

1 green boat

1 hammerhead shark

1 jellyfish

1 pink octopus

2 seaplanes

1 message in bottle

Find each of these objects in the museum.

Find 10 mice hiding in the vegetable patch.

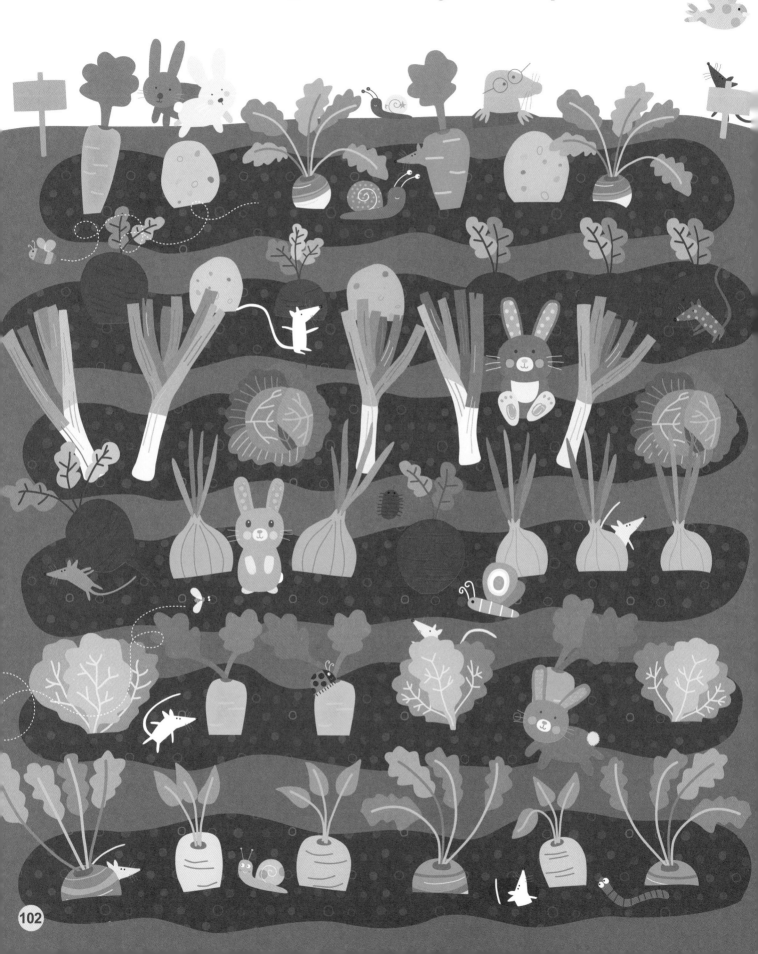

Find the 5 sheep with funky hair styles!

G O !

10 10 10

These gymnasts are working hard! Find...

1 pink ribbon

1 turtle

1 clipboard

4 chalk stands

WORLD CHAMPIONSHIPS

1 gold cup   1 teddy bear   1 red and yellow bag   9 water bottles

Find each of these creatures in the mountains.

Where in the world? Find ...

1 lion

1 kangaroo

1 Taj Mahal

1 panda

1 monkey

1 Big Ben

2 deer

1 whale

Let's get out and about in the city! Find ...

3 lions

1 cat

1 sailor hat

1 green gas pump

 2 traffic lights **1 clock face** **2 monkeys**  **1 whale**

Wow! This concert is great! Find ...

1 green and purple ballon

1 penguin

1 orange cup

3 dark blue balloons

1 pair of earmuffs

1 red and white balloon

1 bear

1 disco ball

How many gold coins are hidden in the captain's cabin?

Fantastic fruit! Find ...

5 strawberries

6 pineapples

8 oranges

1 bear

Let's play hide-and-seek in the attic! Find ...

1 orange box

1 sock

1 T-shirt

1 ghost

1 teacup

1 black cat

1 brown mouse

1 suit of armor

Find each of these at the play center.

119

Answers

Pages 4-5

Pages 6-7

Pages 8-9

30

Page 10

Page 11

Pages 12-13

Pages 14-15

Pages 16-17

Pages 18-19

Page 20-21

Page 22   Page 23

Pages 24-25

Pages 26-27

Pages 28-29

Pages 30-31

Pages 32-33

Pages 34-35

Page 36   Page 37

Pages 38-39

Pages 40-41

Pages 42-43

Page 44   Page 45

Page 46-47

Pages 48-49

Pages 50-51

Page 52　　**Page 53**　　　　**Page 54-55**

Pages 56-57　　　　　**Page 58-59**

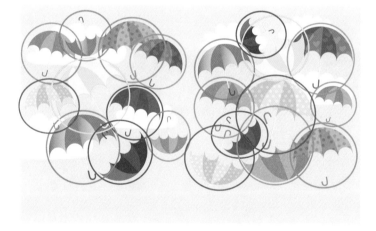

Page 60　　**Page 61**　　　　**Page 62-63**

Pages 64-65

Page 66-67

Pages 68-69

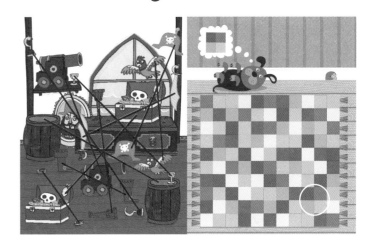

Page 70   Page 71

Page 72-73

Page 74-75

Pages 76-77

Page 78   Page 79

Pages 80-81

Pages 82-83

Pages 84-85

Pages 86-87

Page 88-89

Page 90   Page 91

Pages 92-93

Pages 94-95

Page 96   Page 97

Pages 98-99

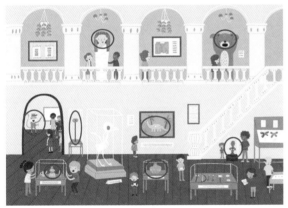

Pages 100-101

Page 102   Page 103

Page 104-105

Page 106-107

Pages 108-109

Pages 110-111

Pages 112-113

Page 114   Page 115

Pages 116-117

Pages 118-119